THE GETAWAY

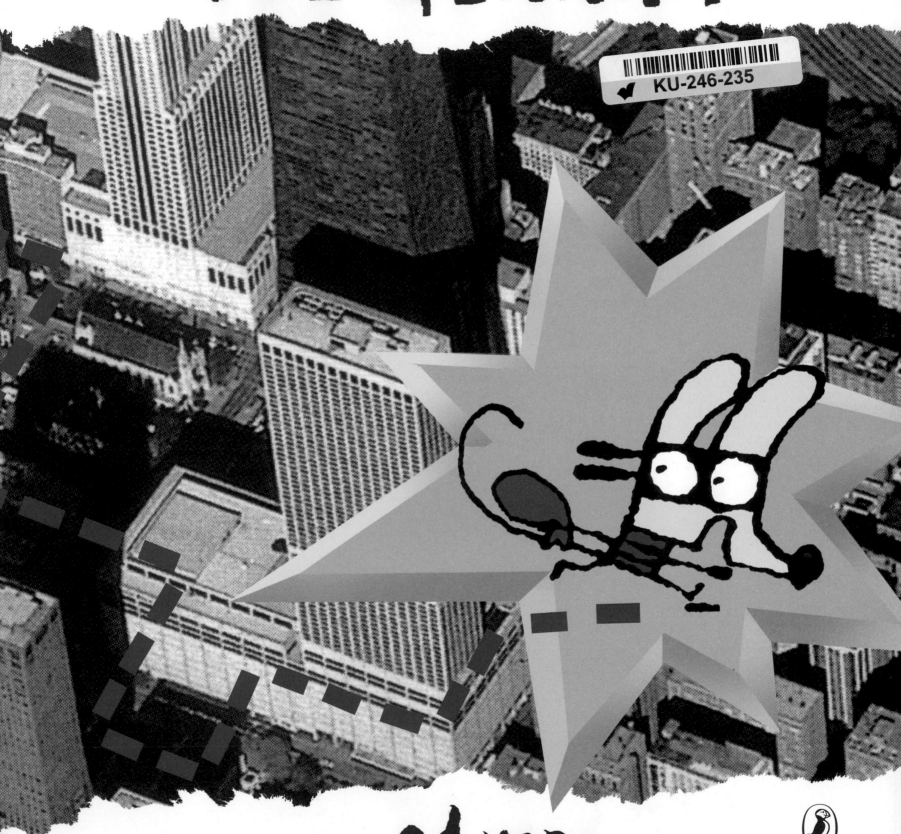

KU-246-235

ed vere

PUFFIN

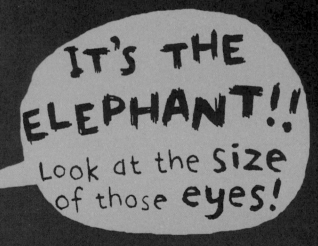

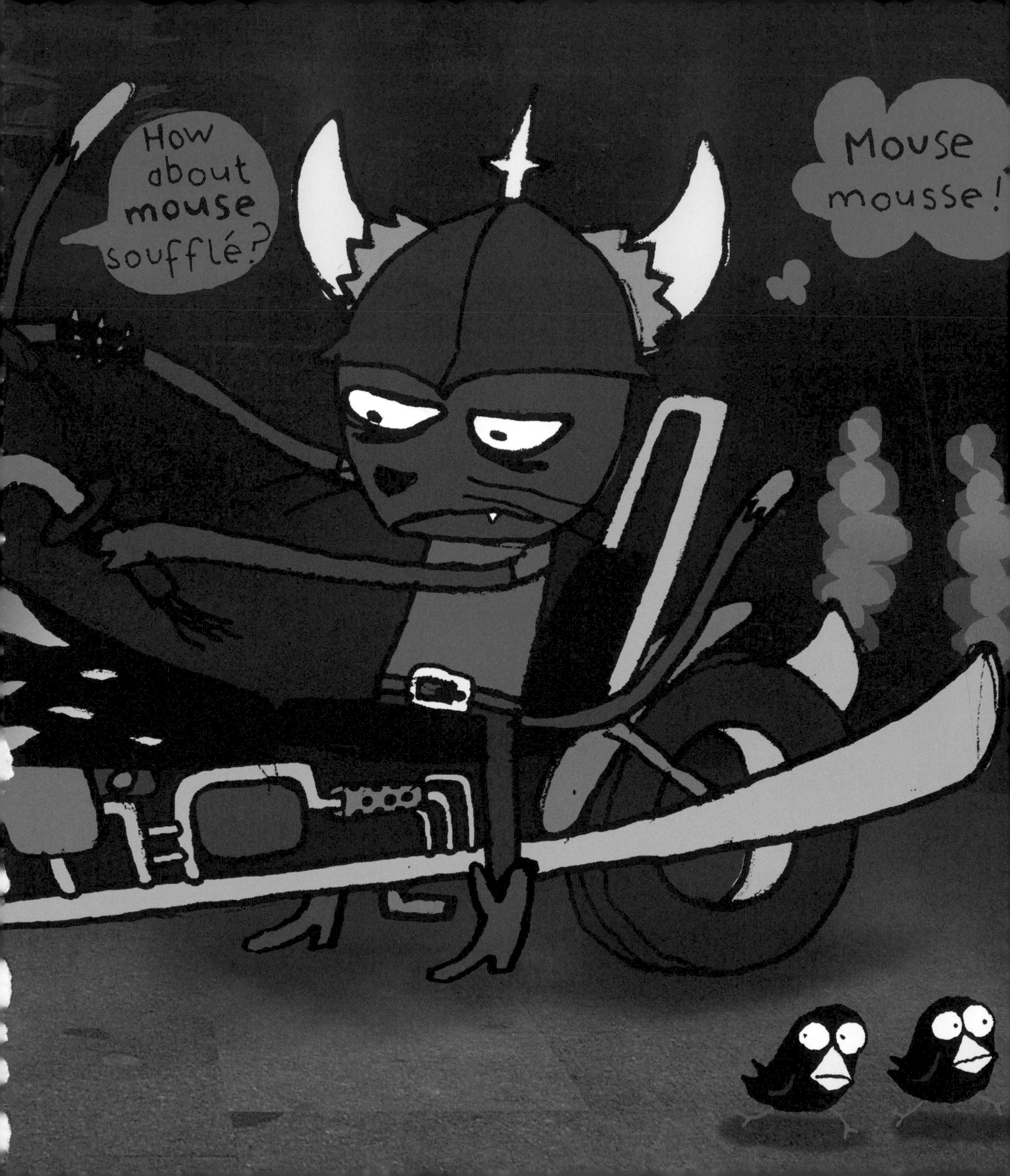
How about **mouse** soufflé?
Mouse mousse!

Hey kid, keep those peepers open! I know you're new to this, but that was a close scrape!

Good Grief, it's that no-good cheese thief, FINGERS McGRAW! Come back here you scoundrel!
No dice mister, you won't get your mitts on me!
?
MAP

5.00PM: THINGS ARE HOTTING UP AND TIME IS RUNNING OUT!
Hey kid, you want a bigger cut or something?!! That was way too close! Remember, just WHISTLE!
Now,
eat
my

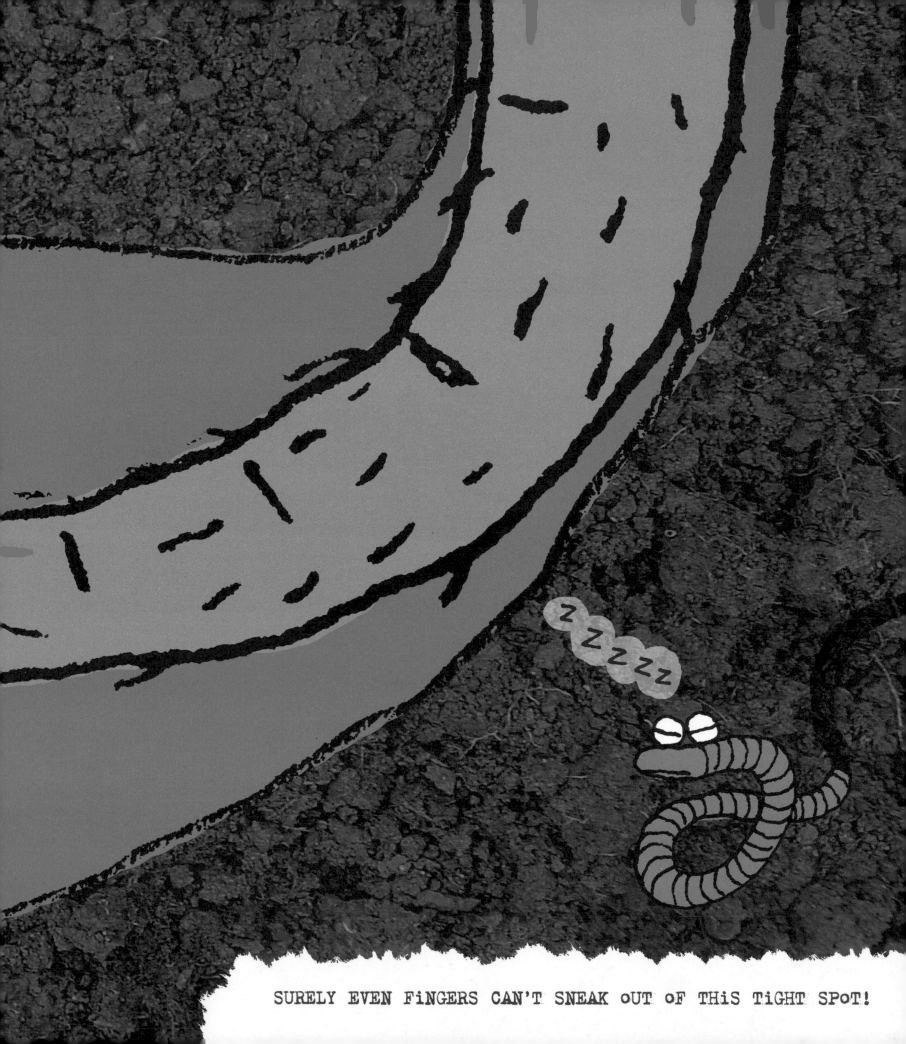

SURELY EVEN FINGERS CAN'T SNEAK OUT OF THiS TiGHT SPoT!

IS THiS THE END FoR FiNGERS...?

...OR iS HE?

THE GETAWAY

PUFFIN BOOKS PRESENTS AN ED VERE PRODUCTION OF "THE GETAWAY"
STARRING FINGERS AS "FINGERS McGRAW" BENICIO del RHINO jr. ROMAN RATANSKI
AND INTRODUCING JUMBO WAYNE jr. III AS "THE LAWMAKER"
FILMED ON LOCATION IN LONDON, BARCELONA, CHICAGO AND BILBAO
FILMED IN MOUSE-O-VISION
WRITTEN AND DIRECTED BY ED VERE

PUFFIN BOOKS
UK | USA | Canada | Ireland | Australia
India | New Zealand | South Africa
Puffin Books is part of the Penguin Random House group of companie
whose addresses can be found at global.penguinrandomhouse.com.

www.penguin.co.uk   www.puffin.co.uk   www.ladybird.co.uk

First published in hardback 2006
Paperback edition published 2007
Reissued 2018
001
Copyright © Ed Vere, 2006
The moral right of the author/illustrator has been asserted
Printed in China
A CIP catalogue record for this book is available from the British Librar
ISBN: 978–0–141–50058–4

All correspondence to: Puffin Books, Penguin Random House Children'
80 Strand, London WC2R 0RL

MIX
Paper from
responsible sources
FSC
www.fsc.org
FSC® C018179

www.edvere.com   @ed_vere

for Bicu

C29 0000 0793 292

sniff

sniff